Tale of A Baseball Dream

Jerry Pearlman

ISBN: 978-0-578-01986-4

Legend has it, that Bubba "The Brute"
Brugosee was heralded, as the "Greatest
Baseball Hero that Ever Lived."
Brugosee had led the New Jersey
Force to six World Championships
in his first seven years with the team.

Table of Contents

CHAPTER 1

Our Story Begins

It was a perfect afternoon in September, and I was pitching balls to Dusty in our local neighborhood park. Dusty was eight-years-old, and full of smiles and energy.

It was getting kind of late, and I was about ready to call it quits, when Dusty hit a groundball just to my right. I dove for the ball, but it trickled past me. Dusty turned 1st base and headed towards 2nd. I grabbed the ball, jumped to my feet, and began to run towards 2nd to try and tag him out. Dusty dove on his belly to try and beat the tag.

"You're out!" I said, as I rolled over to sit up while holding the ball over my head.

"Uh uh, uh uh, Dad--I was safe. You missed me with the ball."

"I am so tired, Dusty! I am so tired. I can't play anymore!"

Dusty then said, "Come on Dad, one more, just one more Dad."

"Okay," I said in a disappointed tone. I fought my way back to my feet and began walking towards where I would stand to pitch him another ball.

I threw him another pitch.

Dusty swung and hit the ball to right field, just clearing the infield in the air.

"Did you see that? Did you see that, Dad? Wow! THAT'S THE GREATEST HIT I'VE EVER SEEN!" Dusty threw his hands in the air, did a little skip, and enthusiastically started running around the bases.

I calmly fell to the ground.

Chapter 1 - Our Story Begins

CHAPTER 2

The Legend

Many years earlier, a New Jersey sports fan was in his living room listening to his radio. He went stomping into the dining room to talk to his wife, as she was putting a casserole dish on the table.

"Did you hear that? Did you hear that, baby? They got rid of 'The Brute.'" The man said to his wife, in a kind of a desperate and non-believing voice. He then turned to face the radio and again said, "They got rid of 'The Brute.' I can't believe it. What are we gonna do now?"

Bubba "The Brute" Brugosee had led the league in the categories of homeruns, runs batted in, and batting average for six of the first seven years he was in the league.

As a pitcher, Brugosee led the league in wins, strikeouts, and innings pitched, all seven years.

"The Brute" had just gotten word that he had been traded from the New Jersey Force, by their owner Larry Shobeling, and his assistant Ralph Schnooberhuber.

That evening, the owners of the New Jersey Force were interviewed on television, and provided all of New Jersey with their explanation, that they regret that they had to let "The Brute" go, but that his better days were behind him.

They proceeded to attempt to paint a bright picture for the future of New Jersey baseball, and reassured the people of New Jersey that they would continue to win many World Championships.

Soon after that, "The Brute" arrived in Cleveland, and appeared very sad and unhappy. The reporters surrounded him and were barraging him with questions.

"The Brute" was half-heartedly answering their questions, when a reporter from the back of the crowd said, "New Jersey says you can no longer play and that they can win without you. They said they dumped their trash on our lawn."

There was then a complete silence in the air.

"The Brute" slowly looked up. It was said that you could then see the glare in his eyes, the intensity in his face, and the veins popping out of his neck.

He then spoke in a slow and very direct voice. "You tell New Jersey, THEY WILL NEVER WIN ANOTHER CHAMPIONSHIP AS LONG AS I LIVE!"

There was then all sorts of stirring and commotion in the crowd.

"The Brute" then spoke again. "You tell New Jersey that Cleveland will dominate the baseball world from this day until the END OF ALL TIME!"

The crowd started an immediate and tremendous uproar.

"The Brute" then climbed into the car that took him through the crowd, which then showed the enthusiasm of a parade! A Dixieland style band was playing music, while following his car down the street.

"The Brute" was finally smiling and waving to everyone, as they headed through the crowd! He stood up in his car, waving his arms in the air with his half-chewed cigar dangling from his mouth. He enthusiastically shook hands with his newly elated fans and reporters, as his car continued in what was then a parade.

Horns were honking, while fans were dancing and shouting with excitement! There were balloons flying, and children skipping along with their dogs, joining the parade!

Chapter 2 - The Legend

CHAPTER 3

Back To Modern Day

It was another beautiful day, and I was again hitting Dusty some grounders in our neighborhood park. Dusty was doing a good job of fielding the grounders.

After about five groundballs Dusty asked, "Can I bat now dad?"

I told Dusty. "It is important to practice on fielding grounders, and catching the ball. The game will be more fun for you if you can become really good on defense. The coach will put you where he thinks the other team will hit the ball, and you get to catch it and get the other team's player out."

I saw Dusty walking quickly back towards 3rd base. He then turned towards me and said, "Okay, okay. I'm ready, Dad." as he pounded his fist into his mitt, and bent his knees in ready position.

I hit him many grounders, and he was very good at cleanly fielding almost every ball that came near him. After a while it started to get dark, and there were no lights in the park. Dusty was totally covered in dirt from his face to his toes. I then hit him a pop up which he caught and threw back to me. Dusty then turned and ran about five steps further away from me, towards the outfield.

He turned towards me, and again got in the "ready" position. I then hit him another grounder.

Dusty scooped it up and said, "No Dad." He kinda threw his hands toward the ground while whining a little. "HIT IT IN THE AIR!"

I sighed, and then hit him another pop up. Dusty caught it, threw it back, and then of course turned and ran further into the outfield.

I then told Dusty, "I think we've played long enough. Let's go. It's getting dark, and I'm getting hungry."

But Dusty talked me into it. "Come on Dad, please, I'm getting really good!"

"Dusty, we're going now!" I clearly told him.

Dusty replied. "Come on, Dad. I need to practice. How am I going to be *great* if I never practice?"

I reluctantly walked back to home plate, threw up another ball, and again hit it to Dusty, who was now standing well into the outfield. Dusty started backing up for the ball, and just as he put up his glove to catch it, he tripped and the ball landed squarely in his mouth. Dusty started screaming at the top of his lungs, while blood was gushing everywhere.

My heart sank into my stomach, as I ran desperately to see if he was okay. I immediately threw him over my shoulder,

and ran back to the house while he was
screaming all the way.

Fortunately, we only lived a few
houses from the park, and Dusty did not
lose any teeth.

CHAPTER 4

Back In Time Again

For many years after Brugosee had been traded to Cleveland, he was a huge success! Cleveland was dominating all of baseball, and winning one World Championship after another!

Meanwhile, the New Jersey baseball team never put forth much of a showing.

The fans of New Jersey did not forget what it had meant for their city to lose "The Brute." The fans became more and more disgruntled each year that passed without making it to the World Championship.

Many years later, "The Brute" died. It has been said that as his soul was flying towards the heavens, New Jersey baseball fans could see his "ghost" spinning violently, while hearing the distinct bass sounding voice of "The Brute" saying, "NEW JERSEY WILL NEVER, EVER, WIN ANOTHER WORLD CHAMPIONSHIP. YOU WILL PAY FOR WHAT YOU DID. YOU WILL PAY FOREVER!"

After his death, Bubba "The Brute" Brugosee was heralded as "The greatest baseball legend of all time!"

CHAPTER 5

Dusty's Early Years

I remember when Dusty was only four-years-old. He was like my shadow, always following me around the house, tossing the tennis ball up in the air and catching it.

Dusty would constantly be nagging me, "Throw me the ball, Dad. Come on, Dad. Throw me the ball."

I would be sitting in our reclining chair in the living room talking on the phone, while Dusty would be climbing on the couch, where he would push off and jump as high and far as he could. I would toss the ball in the air far enough away from him that he'd have to jump and make an outstanding play to catch it. I could swear by the time he was six-years-old, he had made some of the greatest plays that I had ever seen!

CHAPTER 6

Time Went By

When Dusty was 10-years-old, he played 2nd base and sometimes pitched, while in his second year of Little League.

In the first game he ever pitched, Dusty threw a complete game, and won, against a team that had won six straight games. Dusty's team had a one run lead, and he struck out the last batter of the game with the bases loaded.

Dusty went running off the field, threw his glove in the air, and yelled, "I knew I was a good pitcher!"

A pizza party followed, and the kids had an awesome time playing video games, and splashing pizza all over their faces and uniforms!

In the last game of the season, Dusty made a diving play while playing 2nd base. Dusty sprung to his feet, and threw out the runner at home plate. That sparked his team into the playoffs, in another thrilling game to remember.

Soon thereafter, disappointment set in when they called the names of the 10–year-old tournament All Star Team.

Dusty and I sat in the stands with great anticipation, and a strong feeling that his name would be called, for being selected to the team. Dusty heard the names of many of his friends called, but his face fell into his hands as the 14th and final name was called.

I probably felt the exact horrible sinking feeling in my heart that Dusty did that day. I knew a great injustice had taken place. Dusty was an outstanding player, and for him not to be recognized would be something that I was sure he could not understand.

After the silent ride home, Dusty stormed out of the car screaming, "I hate baseball!" as he threw his glove against the wall.

He ran into the house crying and screaming, "I hate baseball. It's not fair, Dad. It's not fair!"

Dusty's face was straight down in his bedspread, as I entered his room.

"It was not fair that you didn't make the All Star Team," I told him. "You are definitely one of the best players. I believe that if you continue to practice baseball, the way you practice now, that you will become a great baseball player, and good things will happen!"

"Let's go to the field, Dad! Let's go. Let's play some baseball!"

Dusty and I went to the field and turned on the lights after everyone had left. I pitched while Dusty hit one ball after another. He was hitting the ball further and further with each pitch, getting closer and closer to hitting the ball near the fence.

Dusty became determined that he was going to be the first 10-year-old to hit the ball over the fence.

Then, like a miracle, Dusty swung as hard as he could, and the ball went flying over the eight foot high "Giant Blue Wall!"

Dusty took off around the bases, skipping, jumping, turning circles, and yelling with excitement, as his hands were flying high in the air. I had an unexplainable feeling in my heart, and almost broke into tears of joy!

"That's it, son! That's it! Don't let it get you down! Don't let anything stop you!"

When Dusty reached home plate, I was there to greet him with a big hug!

I picked him up and swung him around and around!

"I did it, Dad! I did it! I can't believe it! I'm the only 10-year-old to ever hit a ball over the fence! Let's play some more, Dad! We can't stop now! I'm on FIRE! THIS IS THE GREATEST DAY OF MY LIFE!"

"That was SUPER! I never thought I'd see anything like that!" I said as I shook my head back and forth. "We've got to go now. It's getting very late and we need to get home."

"Okay, but can we come back tomorrow?" Dusty asked, as he helped gather the equipment.

"We'll see, Dusty. We'll see."

After we hopped into the car and started heading home, I told Dusty. "Dusty, you have to remember that sometimes the things that happen, that seem to be the most terrible thing in the world at the time, somehow turn out to make our lives better. I think that because you did not make the All Star Team, you will become a much better player than you would have ever been if you had made the team."

I was right! Dusty was determined to prove that he should have made the All Star Team!

It was very peaceful and relaxing to spend time with my son each day after work. I would toss him one pitch after another, until we were watching the sun go down. Dusty was completely inspired to become the best baseball player that ever lived!

CHAPTER 7

The Curse Lives

Back in New Jersey, the fans were still booing and booing their team. The newspapers had deemed the New Jersey Force's inability to win as being due to the "Curse of the Great Brutester!"

The ghost of "The Brute" was sitting on his couch, watching all of the New Jersey fan's disappointments going on below, on his special "swirling cloud TV" in heaven. He was just laughing and laughing, as he watched the fans of New Jersey.

"Do you realize yet, that you really did not know what you were doing when you traded me? Try to mess me around, for your own personal gain?" he said in a spiteful tone of voice. "I don't think so, HAH! Ya'll really MESSED UP BIG TIME! New Jersey will never, ever, ever, be happy again. Are you happy now? And it's all because you think it's okay to mess around with someone that had done so much for you. That was not cool. You shouldn't have done me wrong!" he said as he madly chucked his plate across the heavens in a fit of rage.

"Hey, give them a break." a voice from behind "The Brute" spoke. "It wasn't the people of New Jersey that did you wrong. It was only a couple of pitiful souls that did not appreciate what you had contributed to their team! Give the people of Jersey a break," the voice said, as Tory Clure, a former Hall of Fame Member and Super Legend appeared in the room.

"I think it's time you mind your own business--like you're a really good guy or something." "The Brute" responded.

They both broke out laughing as "The Brute" handed Tory a soda.

"No one, not no one, messes 'The Brute' around. Not when I made that town what it was."

"Okay, okay already. They got it. Cut them some slack already after 43 years." Tory blurted.

"Well, maybe I should give them a break. After all, it has been 43 years of punishment to them. Well, Hmmm...

Maybe I'll think about it." "The Brute" said, as he broke out into a loud and obnoxious laugh.

"You know, Tory. I think I'll let them win the World Championship. Just to show them my heart! I mean it--this year the Force all the way!"

That was the year that the Force needed just one more out to win the World Championship.

It was said that "The Brute" changed his mind, as a routine soft pop up floated what looked to be harmlessly towards Jordie Jenkins the 2nd baseman. If only Jenkins would have caught the ball, the Force would have won the World Championship.

Many New Jersey fans actually swore to seeing the ghost of "The Brute" on the field, as the ball approached Jordie. The story is that "The Brute" gently blew the baseball off course at the exact instant that Jenkins stuck his glove up to catch it. That caused the baseball to move just enough, to bounce off the tip of Jenkins' glove, and fall softly onto the right field grass.

The entire New Jersey area was again in disbelief.

"The Brute" just looked at Tory and threw up his hands, as he returned to his chair, and said. "I just couldn't see those bums cheering and all happy around there."

Tory just rolled his eyes, and walked away shaking his head.

CHAPTER 8

A Real Dream

It was the last day of school of Dusty's 3rd grade year, and we were running late. Dusty grabbed his backpack and jumped in the car, and I backed out of the driveway watching carefully for children walking to school.

Dusty said. "Dad, you won't believe what happened to me last night!"

"What, Dusty?" I asked.

"I was in this awesome baseball game! I was batting with two outs, and we had a guy on 2nd base. And it was SO LOUD! People were yelling and screaming, and going crazy! And the pitcher threw me the ball, and I CRUSHED IT! I CRUSHED IT AS HARD AS I COULD and the ball went flying over this GIANT BLUE WALL! Like the wall I hit my home-run over, at our field, but it was MUCH BIGGER! IT WAS SO UNBELIEVABLE! And all of these people started running onto the field, and jumping up and down. Up and down, Dad. And they were spinning around, and picking each other up, and dancing!"

"That is really neat, Dusty." I said as I kept my eyes on the road.

Dusty continued. "And then there were fireworks, and this GIANT score-board was flashing on and off. It was saying something. But I don't know what!"

"That's a cool dream." I responded.

"No, Dad. It wasn't a dream. It was real. It had to be real. I know it happened!. Hmmm. I guess it had to be a dream. DARN. Bye Dad!"

Dusty then hopped out of the car.

"Bye Dusty! Have a great day. Pay attention in school." I told him, and then took off in a hurry to try and avoid being late for work.

Chapter 8 - A Real Dream

CHAPTER 9

That Summer Flew By

After that summer, Dusty entered the 4th grade, and happened to end up in the same class as Randy, who would later become Dusty's best friend for life.

Randy also loved baseball, and like Dusty, he loved to play all the time. Randy was almost a year older, and a lot bigger than Dusty, and was also a great hitter.

We would all go to the baseball fields for many hours at a time on weekends, and at least one or two other days during the week, to play "homerun derby." Randy usually won, and although Dusty could not hit the ball as far as Randy, he would usually hit almost as many homeruns. They would both always strive to hit more homeruns than the previous time we were there.

The Little League allowed us to turn on the lights at the field, and we often enjoyed playing baseball until late at night! I would hit Dusty and Randy what seemed like *hundreds* of groundballs. Dusty loved for me to hit the ball just far enough away from where he was standing, that he could practice making *unbelievable* diving plays. Randy was happy to play first base, and was not interested in making the *fancy* plays, but would never tire of playing.

At least twice a week, I would also take Dusty and Randy to the batting cages that had pitching machines. The pitching machines helped them by throwing the ball faster than any pitcher they would bat against during the season. I believed strongly in repetition. I knew that if Dusty and Randy practiced batting over and over it would become automatic.

I also encouraged the boys to always work towards improving on the little things, such as keeping their weight on their back foot, while they swung at the pitch. I saw many young players who thought they just were not good hitters, when all they really needed were some small adjustments. I'm sure that Dusty and Randy became sick of hearing, *Little things make a big difference*! That however, is the most important advice I could ever give any baseball player!

I felt a strong sense to spend a lot of time working with the boys on their game. I believed that would give them the best opportunity to develop their skills, and have more successful experiences playing baseball.

Dusty and Randy were inseparable. They were true friends! Randy would spend almost every weekend with us. He and Dusty would be chasing each other through the house, yelling and screaming, wrestling, playing video games, and eating pizza!

I took them many Saturday nights to the Starlite Bowl, which was a place to bowl while listening to loud music and watching laser lights. They would eat nachos, French fries, ice cream, and almost every other junk food you could think of until they dropped!

We went to movies, carnivals, and theme parks! We went fishing, camping, and to awesome water parks! We were having the times of our lives!

I had been promising Dusty since he was about six-years-old that when we had the money to get the fence in the backyard fixed, he could have a dog. I'm sure that Dusty had given up on that day ever coming.

I surprised him one afternoon near the end of summer. Randy, Dusty, and I jumped in the car and headed to the dog pound.

We had looked at every dog there at least three or four times, before we finally decided on a homely looking puppy that was half lab and half golden retriever. Dusty knew right away that his dog's name would be Homer!

Somehow, Homer turned out to be the greatest dog that ever lived! He was shy at first, but became very loving and playful. It was great to have this wonderful dog that was always happy to see us!

We never formally trained Homer, but he had a very good sense of knowing what we wanted him to do most of the time. Homer was extremely frisky and friendly. He was also very cuddly. He quickly became such a part of our family that it seemed as though he had been with us forever!

Dusty loved his dog!

CHAPTER 10

More Baseball

The following spring, Dusty was 11-years-old, and played his first year in the Little League Majors. He was paired with 11 and 12-year-olds.

Dusty had a great year; playing the entire season at shortstop, and his team won first place! Dusty contributed to his team's success by coming up with many clutch hits, helping them win games.

Dusty's batting average was .550, which was the 3rd best in the league, and he also played excellent shortstop through-out the season!

Dusty was again overlooked, and did not make the All Star Team. This time, however, Dusty was not very disappointed about not being selected. After all, there were only a couple of 11-year-olds that made the team.

Dusty was still inspired, and continued to practice all the time! He was determined to not let anything stop him from being great!

Dusty had another great year when he was 12, during his final year in Little League. He was definitely a star player, and the season came down to the final game, which his team had to win to make the playoffs.

It seemed like every coach, player, and family attended this final game of the year! We could feel the excitement, as the game was tied in the final inning, when Dusty came to bat with the bases loaded and two outs.

Dusty crushed the first pitch off of the top of the left field wall to win the game!

That year, Dusty was finally acknowledged and honored, by being selected to the All Star Team! He was incredibly proud as he walked from the stands to home plate to pick up his trophy after they announced his name!

Dusty played Pony League baseball the next couple of years, and continued to excel!

Our lives did not seem to change much during those years. Dusty remained close friends with Randy. Homer also stayed a very big part of our lives.

I continued to strongly encourage Dusty to keep up his love of playing baseball, and his strong practice routines. I believed that his *heart* and relentless determination made him *special*.

CHAPTER 11

High School

Before you knew it, Dusty began high school. He went to Centerwood High, and seemed to like it.

Dusty tried out, and made the junior varsity baseball team in the fall. He had a relatively small body type, and was not taken very seriously as a player that could have much of an impact to help the team. Dusty played very well his freshman and sophomore years.

When he began his junior year, he still only weighed 136 pounds, and when it came to lifting weights, he was the weakest player on the team. It seemed that no matter how hard he tried, Dusty could not do much to impress the coaches, or any of the other players! After all, Dusty was far from having an *intimidating* presence.

Finally, In the last game of the season of his junior year, Dusty came to bat in his team's last at bat of a tie game. Dusty ripped the first pitch over the left field fence!

What was so unbelievable is the fact that he hit the ball so far, and that no one actually saw the ball land, but only could see a flock of birds flying away in the background! For some mysterious reason, the ball appeared to never come down! The entire team went to search for the ball so Dusty could keep it as a souvenir, but the ball had completely disappeared, and was never found.

Dusty's teammates were finally excited about having Dusty on the team. They were telling everyone that Dusty had hit the longest homerun in Centerwood history!

I told Dusty that nothing could keep him from being a professional ballplayer! I told him that he was the greatest *pure* quality player that I had ever seen, and that he had the guts, determination and skills to become one of the greatest players of all time!

Chapter 12

Disaster Strikes

Everything came to a screeching halt! In the summer before Dusty's senior year, I had been diagnosed with cancer. The cancer had eaten me away so badly, that I only had a couple of months to live.

That was a total crusher to Dusty. I kept trying to get him to continue with his life, but he was very distraught. He did not step onto the field his senior year, and did not even pick up a bat. Dusty seemed to have lost interest in everything.

I hung on until September. I made sure that Dusty knew that he was my greatest

love, and that he somehow would no longer need me. I let him know that God had
someone in mind for him, to replace our
relationship. I told him that the only thing
he needed to do was to continue to be the
great kid he already was.

I gracefully passed with Dusty close
by my side.

CHAPTER 13

Desperation Emerges

Dusty's whole being was taken over by an uproar of emotions. He had very strong feelings of anger towards me. I had promised him that he would be great, and he believed me strongly enough to dedicate his whole life to becoming a great baseball player. His anger was directed at me because he believed that I was not truthful with him about his potential to become a great player. He then felt that he had no future.

For some strange reason beyond comprehension, on the stormy day of my funeral, Dusty threw his bat and a bucket of baseballs in the back of his car, and drove to his old Pony League field, where we had spent so many days practicing. Dusty was completely out of control and in a desperate rage as he tromped through the mud, carrying his bat and the baseballs while heading towards home plate. Dusty dropped the bag, picked up the bat, and tossed a ball in the air.

"Why did you tell me I was a great player?!" He yelled, as he swung and knocked the ball over the left field fence.

"I'm really not that good, Dad!" he shouted, as he hit another baseball over the fence, and on top of the shack behind it.

"I am really mad at you, Dad!" he screamed, as he crushed another ball completely over the shack, and against the brick wall of the four story building that stood behind the shack.

"You ruined my life, Dad!" Dusty shouted, as he threw up another ball and this time *blasted* it all the way onto the parking lot, on top of the four story building!

"What am I going to do now?!" Dusty cried out, as he swung and ripped another ball that again landed in the same parking lot on top of the building.

"It's just not fair. You shouldn't of died, Dad. You shouldn't of died," he pleaded, and then crumbled to his knees, as his face fell into his hands.

Chapter 13 - Desperation Emerges

CHAPTER 14

A Real Twist

"Is this yours? Is this yours, Sonny?" A gentle voice asked as Dusty slowly lifted his head to look.

Dusty then saw a frail looking man, about 70-years-old standing in front of him.

The man was holding a drenching wet baseball in his hand, with his arm stretched towards Dusty, as if he were gesturing to give Dusty his ball back.

"I don't know," Dusty replied, as he gradually lowered his head back into his hands, as if he didn't even realize that someone was standing there.

"This is the ball I've been looking for my whole life." the man said. "I wish I had found it sooner, but better late than never." the man uttered as he smiled and proceeded to toss the ball slightly up in the air and catch it.

"What's wrong, kid?" the man wanted to know, with a look of complete concern.

"My dad died. He died and left me nothing--nothing but a big disappointment."

"I know one thing you have, Sonny. The most unbelievable bat I've ever seen." the man said in a direct tone.

"Yeah? Well that's what my dad use to tell me too. And he was just a liar!"

"I'm not a liar, Sonny. I'm a pro scout for the New Jersey Force. Have been for 37 years. I've never seen anyone hit a ball like that! And you know the funny thing, I had almost given up. I almost gave up being a scout. I was beginning to think I just wasn't any good. You know when you try as hard as I have at something, and you've been unsuccessful for 37 years, you begin to wonder." the man said, as he was shaking his head while deep in thought.

"And you know the funny thing," the man again said, "I'm not even supposed to be here. I'm supposed to be in Philadelphia today. I was having a terrible day. I got on an airplane at the wrong terminal, and ended up in Houston. I decided.

What the heck, if I'm in Houston, I might as well surprise my Aunt Bessie and drop in on her. You know it's kind of funny, but I think it's been about 37 years since I've last seen her." he said, while shaking his head as if he were in disbelief of his own story.

"I rented a car when I got to Houston, and began driving towards Aunt Bessie's house, when it started raining so hard I couldn't see. Somehow, I got lost and turned down this street, to try and find a place I could stop to get my bearings straight. For what seemed like no reason at all, I decided to go into that building over there." He stopped and pointed towards the entrance of the building behind the left field fence.

"I couldn't find a parking place until I got all the way to the top floor of the parking lot. I got out of my car and started running towards the building to try and keep from getting too wet. A darn baseball comes flying out of nowhere, and knocks the stupid umbrella out of my hand. I thought, *WHAT THE HECKFIRE WAS THAT!?*

"I walked on over to the edge of the building, and looked down just in time to see you throw up another ball and hit it straight at me. I couldn't believe my eyes! I just stood there in disbelief, while the darn thing came straight at me. You darn near killed me, Sonny! I jumped out of the way just in time, or we wouldn't be having this conversation!"

"Will Parker!" the man said, as he put out his right hand for Dusty to shake. "I'm Will Parker, and I've just seen what I waited my whole life to see! God sure does work in mysterious ways," the man said, as he again shook his head in disbelief, while looking at the baseball he was holding.

"Do you mind if I keep this?" he asked, while still shaking his head and looking at the baseball.

"Sure, go ahead." Dusty mumbled softly, while still hanging his head towards the ground.

"What is your name, son?"

"Dusty. Dusty Hunter."

"Pleasure to meet you, Dusty, Dusty Hunter!" Will said, as he again shook Dusty's hand.

"You wouldn't mind too much playing for the New Jersey Force would you, Dusty Hunter? I mean, it would kinda help me out of a jam."

Dusty looked up in total disbelief.

Mr. Parker went on to explain. "You see, Dusty, I'm in kind of a funny situation. I've been a scout like I said, for the team for 37 years, and they kind of think of me now as a joke. It's kind of to the point where I'm just there to be there. You know what I mean?"

"Kind of. I think so." Dusty responded, while looking a little baffled.

"I've always, always wanted to prove my worth as a scout, but I just about had come to the conclusion that it just wasn't meant to be. At least up until about 10 minutes ago! You see, Dusty, I've never really discovered a player that has done much to make a difference in the outcome of our season."

"Anyway, you see, we haven't won a World Championship now in some ninety or so years. That is, give or take a decade or two. I have this very strong feeling that I am not just standing here talking to you by accident." Will said, as he closed his left eye, and looked up towards the heavens, again shaking his head.

Will turned back towards Dusty, and continued. "Right now we are only three games out of first place, with 14 games left in the regular season. We need you Dusty. We need you to help us." Again, Will looked up at the sky, this time shaking his head slightly up and down several times in a quick motion, appearing to be very deep in thought.

Chapter 14 - A Real Twist

Chapter 15

Preparation Meets Opportunity

Will had more pull in the New Jersey organization than he realized. Dusty was in a New Jersey uniform in only seven days. The Force was now only two games out of the playoff picture, with nine games left in the season. The manager of the Force at the time, believed in miracles, and after hearing Parker's story of how he discovered Dusty, he did not hesitate to put Dusty in the lineup the day he arrived.

Dusty played with the same excitement as he did when he was 10-years-old! He made one unbelievable play after another while playing centerfield. Dusty seemed to knock in a runner every time he batted, and continued to play fantastically for the remainder of the season.

The New Jersey Force did not lose another game during the regular season, and coasted into the playoffs, winning their division by three full games. The Force ended up playing the New Mexico Brawlers in the 1st round of the playoffs. The Force could do no wrong as they convincingly won the series three games to one!

Dusty had again contributed by playing phenomenal baseball, and the rest of the team was also playing with great confidence!

Next, the Force had to take care of their number one nemesis, the Cleveland

Gangsters. New Jersey, again, could do no wrong, as they won the series in just four games! The fans of New Jersey were going crazy, as they were now going to the World Championship!

That's when something strange started to happen. It was almost like the excitement of making it to the World Championship lasted only a few minutes, and then the realization set in that New Jersey cannot win a World Championship.

The players and coaches were of course trying to stay positive, but everyone could feel that a fate beyond their control would again, somehow put an end to their hopes and dreams.

CHAPTER 16

Uh Oh. Here We Go Again.

"The Brute" was having a soda with Todd Blevins; another previous Hall of Fame player; and Tory Clure. The conversation of course turned to the current World Championship. Blevins was trying to convince "The Brute" that it was about time that he finally let the Force win the Championship.

While they were talking, "The Brute" thought he felt the strange presence of another "ghostly" character in the room. "The Brute" held up his soda and looked at it kind of funny, and then shook his head as if telling himself that it was just the soda.

"The Brute" then snapped out of his daze when he heard Tory say, "Have you heard about the new kid? He's really something. The kid is looking like he's destined to lead them to win the Championship."

"Ain't no one gonna help New Jersey win the Championship. Quit being funny!" "The Brute" insisted.

CHAPTER 17

Here We Go!

It was the Force and the Detroit Destroyers lined up for the *big one*.

The Destroyers were quite a story themselves, and also had a "jinx" of their own. Although, it had nowhere near the notoriety of "The Curse of the Great Brutester."

The series was a classic battle, which was very well played. The Destroyers took the first two games using sound pitching, defense, and timely hitting.

The Force bounced back and won the next three games in a row by each player contributing with outstanding defense, and clutch hitting. The Force was just one win away from winning the World Championship, and breaking the infamous "spell!"

The stage was set, and the whole world was watching with great anticipation, knowing that the Force had been this close before.

The game was also well played, and the score was tied with no score in the bottom of the 9th inning, in Detroit. The Destroyers led off the bottom of the 9th with a base hit up the middle, and advanced the runner to 2nd base with a bunt.

The next batter grounded to 2nd base for the second out, which advanced the runner to 3rd base.

With two outs and the crowd roaring, the next batter hit a routine pop up just over the infield, which hung in the air long enough for Dusty to get there. Dusty lost his focus for one split second, glancing towards where he thought he heard a voice and the ball hit the ground right beside him.

The Destroyers had just won the game! That seemed to be the one most tragic moment in baseball history!

Everyone then knew that history was about to repeat itself, and that the Force had again blown their opportunity to break the "evil curse," by one split second. Everyone was going crazy, and everyone felt assured they had just witnessed another episode of "The Curse of the Great Brutester!"

Dusty was totally out of it. He was like a boxer who was just knocked completely senseless. Dusty realized the magnitude of what had just happened. He could not believe that he had spent his whole life preparing for this miserable destiny!

Coach Bradley came to Dusty and tried to bring him back to some sort of normal being. Dusty could not seem to respond.

Chapter 18

The Brutester Rules Again.

Game seven was played in New Jersey on a cold and wintry type of day. It was 49 degrees at game time, and the wind was swirling in every direction. It had seemed as if "The Brute" was in a rage, and completely in charge of the turbulence.

There was a strong sense of gloom in the air. Game seven was another pitcher's duel. John Ragland for the Force was outstanding in his first eight innings, and likewise, the Destroyer's starting pitcher did not give up any threats of a score.

In the top of the 9th, Bobby Nierdorf hit a line drive off of the right hand of Ragland, which jammed his index finger. Ragland could not pitch and Coach Bradley waved in Dusty from centerfield!

"Dusty. I'm counting on you. The entire population of New Jersey is depending on you. You are a winner. Will didn't just happen to end up in the exact spot you hit a baseball that day, for no reason. I believe in you!" Coach Bradley said, as he handed Dusty the ball before slowly walking back to the dugout.

With a runner on 1st and nobody out, Dusty could not throw a strike. Dusty walked the next two batters on eight consecutive pitches, and the situation looked completely bleak.

On Dusty's next pitch, Bart Hankstrom ripped a line drive double into the left centerfield gap, driving in two runs. The fans started heading towards the exits, as the Destroyers then led 2-0.

Somehow, Dusty was not shaken after the double, and seemed to settle down and gained his strength. Dusty struck out the next three batters on nine consecutive pitches, but it surely appeared to be too little, too late.

The presence of "The Curse" had never felt stronger. The Force was down to their final at bat. The Destroyer's pitcher easily retired the first batter, with a groundball right back to the mound.

The next batter beat out an infield hit on a slow roller to third. Buster Maronahan was promptly hit by the next pitch.

That brought Dusty to the plate with a chance to win the game with a homerun, or possibly ground into a double play to end the season, and again break the hearts of New Jersey loyal fans.

You are the miracle this town has waited for all these years! Dusty thought he heard a voice. He stepped out of the batters box, and stretched his arms and legs, before he stepped back in the box.

The first pitch was a strike right down the heart of the plate, as Dusty just watched as it went by. Dusty checked his swing on the next pitch that was inside and it glanced off his bat into foul territory for strike two.

Dusty again stepped out of the batter's box to focus on the situation while he tightened up his batting gloves. Dusty then pictured his dad telling him how great he was. He recalled the first time he met Will. He remembered how much he wanted Will to not feel bad about himself anymore.

Dusty stepped back in the batter's box. The next pitch was a fastball headed straight towards the outside corner. Dusty watched and waited until the last possible split second.

Dusty *exploded!*

He crushed a monster, towering shot to right centerfield, clearing the entire stadium! Fireworks began exploding, and Dusty could see the excitement of the fans jumping over the rails and onto the field.

Apparently, all of the fans that had started to leave when Jersey went behind in the 9th had turned around to witness the finale! The entire field was quickly swarming with ecstatic New Jersey fans as Dusty rounded the bases! There were many tears of joy. Dusty could clearly see in the faces of the fans what it meant for them to be a part of this historical moment; he then jumped in the air and landed on home plate!

Dusty saw everything vividly, as if it were in slow motion. He looked up at the scoreboard, which was then flashing:

THE CURSE IS BROKEN!
THE CURSE IS BROKEN!
THE CURSE IS BROKEN!

The scoreboard then showed a picture of "The Brute," spinning, while fading away in the background, until he completely disappeared!

Dusty looked to the heavens as the fans of the Force carried him around the field!

Chapter 18 - The Brutester Rules Again

Contact The Author

You can contact the author at:

taleofabaseball@aol.com

CPSIA information can be obtained at www.ICGtesting.com
Printed in the USA
BVOW010413300113

311952BV00010B/414/P

9 781427 650641